Live the Adventure!

The Pit—the underground headquarters of the G.I. Joe Team—is your new home. That's because you are about to become its newest member.

Your code name: Outlaw.

Your major talent: Quick thinking under pressure.

Your assignment: Strategy Specialist.

A G.I. Joe Team is about to go into action against the evil forces of COBRA Command. The mission will not be an easy one. You will need to use your special disguise and espionage skills to make sure it is a *successful* one!

Follow the directions at the bottom of each page. Then make your decision about what to do next.

If you make the right decisions, the G.I. Joe Team will score a triumph over COBRA and you will be recognized as a hero. If you make the wrong choices—you'll wish you never left the Pit!

Good luck, Outlaw. Begin your mission on page 1.

G.I. JOE

OPERATION: DEATH STONE

BY BARBARA & SCOTT SIEGEL

BALLANTINE BOOKS ● NEW YORK

RLI: VL: Grades 5 + up
       IL: Grades 6 + up

Copyright © 1986 by Hasbro, Inc.
G.I. JOE$_{TM}$: A trademark of Hasbro, Inc.
FIND YOUR FATE$_{TM}$: A trademark of Random House, Inc.

Library of Congress Catalog Card Number: 85-91208

ISBN 0-345-32936-8

Illustrated by David Henderson

Cover Art by Hector Garrido

Interior Design by Gene Siegel

Editorial Services by Parachute Press, Inc.

Manufactured in the United States of America

First Edition: March 1986

FIND YOUR FATE...

#6

G.I. JOE

OPERATION: DEATH STONE

Two hundred feet below the surface of the Pacific Ocean, a U.S Navy submarine is traveling at top speed to an unknown destination. At least the destination is unknown until Duke, Acting First Sergeant of the G.I. Joe Team, calls a briefing session in the sub's torpedo room. Attending this briefing is a specially selected group chosen for this team. Included are Recondo, a jungle specialist; Roadblock, a heavy machine gunner with a taste for gourmet food; and Snake-Eyes, who's a black belt in twelve styles of martial arts. There's also Blowtorch, a fire expert; Gung-Ho, the toughest marine alive; Mutt, who brings his dog, Junkyard, on every mission, and *you*. Your code name is Outlaw. You got that handle because you never let a few rules stand in the way of accomplishing your mission.

You're glad that Duke has finally decided to fill you in on your next assignment. After three days of being cooped up in this submarine, you're itching for action.

And you're about to start scratching that itch.

The navy personnel close the door behind them and leave the room. Now it's empty, except for your team and the ominous racks of deadly torpedos.

"All right," Duke says, pulling out a map. "This is where we're going, guys—Blood Island."

Turn to page 2.

1

Duke glances around the torpedo room. His expression is all business.

"Just a few short days ago," he explains, "a meteor landed on Blood Island. Our scientists are certain that the meteor was composed of a very rare element—kiladeium." He stops for a moment.

"This kiladeium may be rare," offers Blowtorch, "but what does it have to do with us?"

"I'll tell you," replies Duke. "When even microscopic traces of the element are mixed with certain other metals and heated to fifteen hundred degrees, an alloy is created that is virtually indestructible. There wasn't very much natural kiladeium on the earth, not enough for even one tank. That is, there wasn't until this meteor dropped in on us. But now there's enough for a whole army of tanks."

"I see," you say slowly. "Whoever gets that kiladeium off of Blood Island will be completely impregnable to attack because no bullets or bombs of any kind can penetrate the stuff."

"Exactly," Duke says, then pauses for a moment to make sure you are all paying close attention. He continues, "Our deadliest enemy, COBRA, is aware of this meteor's existence. Our intelligence reports that COBRA Commander is sending a battalion of Crimson Guards to find it. And there's a possibility that Destro and the Baroness are in on this one too."

....

Brace yourself for what's coming next and go on to page 3.

You and your buddies exchange glances. This assignment is going to be tough—very tough. Destro, a freelance weapons manufacturer who sells his wares to the highest bidder, hates the G.I. Joe Team. He'd do anything to see you all destroyed. And the Baroness, who is never completely loyal to either COBRA Commander or Destro, is one of the nastiest intelligence specialists in the business. Backed by a Crimson Guard battalion, they'll be fierce.

"And one more thing," Duke says. "Watch out for the locals. Blood Island is inhabited by a tribe of natives who don't take kindly to trespassers. They shrink the heads of unwanted guests, and I'm not talking about psychiatrists."

At that moment the submarine's Klaxon rings, signaling that the ship is going to surface. The captain's voice comes over the loudspeaker: "Landing party, prepare to debark."

"That's us," says Duke.

....
Spring into action. Turn to page 5.

Slowly, you let the bamboo tree back up and the Baroness, holding on to the other end, is lifted out of the quicksand. When the tree is straight again, she slides down its trunk to stand next to you.

"When that dog started barking," she says with a shudder, "I thought it was Destro coming to kill me."

"There are a lot of people who'd like to see you dead," you say, "but I didn't know Destro was one of them. Why is he after you?"

"Because," she replies with an arrogant smile, "when he tried to take the meteor fragments for himself, I stole them and got away!"

"*You have the kiladeium?*" you ask with astonishment.

"That's what I said," she answers. But the Baroness is a well-known liar.

"If that's true," you counter, "then where are the rocks?"

"After I ran away from Destro, I fell into that quicksand. The meteor fragments are in a bag that sank to the bottom."

Do you believe her?

....

If you think the Baroness might be telling the truth, turn to page 33.

If you think she's lying, turn to page 46.

4

Within a few minutes you and the rest of the G.I. Joe Team leave the safety of the submarine on a rubber raft. You paddle toward an ominous little island. The terrain looks tough. In the center of the island stand towering mountains and a smoking volcano. A deep, impenetrable forest seems to start right at the shoreline. From your vantage point in the raft, you can see no sign of a meteor explosion or a crater.

And when you reach the beach, you find just two faint trails. One of them seems to lead toward the mountains. The other heads off into the thick jungle.

Which one will take you to the meteor crater ...and which one will take you to your death?

If you choose to follow the trail heading up toward the mountains, turn to page 8.

If you choose to follow the trail heading deeper into the jungle, turn to page 10.

Your team can't think of anything they'd enjoy more than knocking out a battalion of Crimson Guards in the privacy of an isolated jungle. You gag the Baroness so she can't give any warning, and then you and the rest of the team follow Recondo to the spot where he saw COBRA Commander's army.

You're deep in the jungle, off the trail, with a clear view of more than a hundred of COBRA's crack troops. There are probably another hundred of them on the other side of the trail. They would have caught you in a deadly crossfire had you fallen into their trap. But now they're in *your* trap!

Go get them on page 7.

It's time for your little ambush to begin. The whole team is staring at Duke and his Colt .45, waiting for his signal to open fire.

Recondo's finger is on the trigger of his M-79 grenade launcher. Roadblock has the enemy in the sights of his M-2 Browning .50 caliber heavy machine gun. Blowtorch is just burning to scorch the enemy with his M-7 flamethrower. Mutt has a fresh clip in his M-16, and it's set on full automatic. Snake-Eyes has a bead on a Crimson Guard officer with his Uzi machine gun.

And you've got a clear field of fire at a whole column of Crimson Guards with your auto pistol.

If it's war COBRA wants, then it's war they're going to get!

Ready, aim ... turn to page 53!

It's just a short hike through the dense jungle before you reach the base of a huge cliff.

"Haul out the climbing gear," orders Duke.

Within a few minutes, the whole team is outfitted with thick, heavy ropes and grappling hooks. Mutt, as always, packs his pooch, Junkyard, into his rucksack and prepares to climb with the added weight of his best friend.

You throw your hooks up to the top of the cliff until they catch on something strong enough to hold your weight. Then, with eight ropes dangling down the side of the rock wall, you all begin to climb.

"Great way to start a vacation," jokes Recondo, who loves a tough climb.

But when you're halfway to the top of the cliff, who should appear above, standing over your ropes, but Destro, the Baroness, and a slew of COBRA Commander's Crimson Guards.

One by one, they are pulling out their sharp knives and getting ready to cut your ropes!

Don't just hang around, go on to page 9.

Though you've barely begun your mission, you're already about to die—and since you're dangling off the side of a cliff by a rope, you can't even fight back! But you've still got a chance to get out of this... maybe.

On your left you see a shadowy crevice in the rock wall, and it just might be a cave opening. If you're right, and you and the rest of the team could swing over there in time, you could save yourselves from a "crashing" defeat.

But you have another choice. There's a boulder sitting on a rock ledge twenty-five feet away. You could take the extra climbing rope you carry over your shoulder and try to lasso it. Then it wouldn't matter if Destro and his cohorts cut your other rope. But you've got to decide fast!

If you think your best chance is to swing for the shadowy crevice, hoping that you'll find a cave there, turn to page 13.

If you think your best chance is to try to lasso the boulder with your spare rope, turn to page 17.

9

The trail into the jungle is overgrown with every imaginable type of tropical plant. The only way for the team to make any progress is to hack a way through the steaming rain forest with machetes.

But your team keeps on going deeper and deeper into the jungle. Soaked with sweat, being eaten alive by mosquitoes, you start to think that maybe trying the mountain trail would have been a better idea. Even Recondo looks as if he needs a breather. But then you suddenly hear a woman's cry for help!

At top speed, you fight your way through the jungle until you burst into a clearing. And there, of all people, is the Baroness! She's sinking fast into a pool of quicksand.

"Please! Help me!" she pleads.

"Watch out, she's not likely to be alone. This looks like a trap," Duke says. "Recondo, Mutt, Snake-Eyes, you guys keep watch on the far side of the clearing. Roadblock, Blowtorch, Gung-Ho," he continues, "you guys watch our back trail. I'll make contact with the sub."

"What about me?" screams the Baroness.

"Oh, yeah," says Duke slowly. "Outlaw, see what you can do about that lady's predicament."

Come on, she's still sinking. Turn to page 12 quickly.

You turn toward the treacherous Baroness, who is up to her waist in quicksand.

"I get all the dirty jobs," you mutter. But it's more than a dirty job—it's a dangerous one. Your instincts tell you that this is some kind of trick. But what if it isn't? You can't let anyone, even someone as rotten as the Baroness, die like this. Just the same, you know that you'd better be careful.

With that thought in mind, should you throw her a rope and pull her out of the quicksand? Or should you bend a bamboo tree down so she can reach it and pull herself up out of the bog?

If you choose to throw the Baroness a rope, turn to page 62.

If you choose to bend a bamboo tree down into her grasp, turn to page 25.

Hanging off the side of a cliff by a rope is no picnic, especially if your enemies are armed and waiting for you at the top. You decide to get off that rope as fast as you can.

Like Tarzan, you swing toward the shadowy opening in the rock face. If there isn't a cave opening there, you're going to smash into the side of the cliff. But what have you got to lose?

"Follow me!" you call out to the others. Because they don't have anything to lose either, they do as you say.

And miracle of miracles, *there is a cave!*

Before Destro and his evil allies can cut through your thick climbing ropes, you scramble inside the dark cave entrance.

Nobody has a flashlight, but Blowtorch solves that problem. "Need a light?" he asks calmly, and suddenly the cave is illuminated by the flare of his flamethrower.

You all move deeper into the gloom, hoping to find an exit from this bleak place. Getting away from Destro isn't going to do you much good if you end up rotting in some old cave.

But it looks as if luck is with you again. There, up ahead, you see a light. You can smell fresh air. . . .

You rush out of the cave—and run right into a small army of fierce-looking natives!

....

Well, aren't you curious? Turn to page 21.

You peer into the thick, gloomy jungle. Destro, the Baroness, and the Crimson Guards are in there somewhere, fleeing with the rocks. But you've got the best clue just waiting for you to decipher.

"Let's try to crack that coded message," you say. "If we can do it, we've got a chance to sniff out COBRA Commander as well as Destro and the rocks."

"One thing seems pretty clear," says Recondo. "COBRA Commander is telling Destro to be at a specific place with those rocks on Saturday."

"Sure," says Snake-Eyes, "but where?"

You slowly recite the message from memory: "Wrestle rocks to Saturday's 25,000 screamers."

"Got any ideas?" asks Duke.

"Who or what is a screamer?" wonders Gung-Ho. "Maybe some jungle animal," he suggests.

"Uh-uh," you say. "We're already in the jungle, and COBRA Commander wants Destro to meet him someplace else. I think the 'screamers' are people!"

"Twenty-five thousand people?" Mutt asks.

"Could be," you reply. "Maybe COBRA is sending Destro to some sort of place that holds 25,000 people."

"That doesn't help much," complains Mutt. "There must be at least two hundred places in the world that can hold 25,000 people."

Don't let a tiny detail like that stop you, Outlaw. Go on to page 15.

14

You definitely need more information if you're going to decipher COBRA Commander's coded message to Destro.

Duke coolly gets on his walkie-talkie and calls the submarine. "Skipper," he says, "would you run a computer check and tell me how many arenas, stadiums, amphitheaters, and the like there are in the world that can seat a crowd of 25,000?"

A few minutes later the sub's captain calls back and says: "There are one hundred and ninety-nine different places throughout the world that hold 25,000 or more people."

....

Don't get held up by that piece of information. Turn to page 16.

15

Mutt can't help but smile at his close guess. But he doesn't smile for long.

"There are, however," continues the sub's captain, "only fifteen places in the whole world that hold *exactly* 25,000."

You look at the cryptic message in Duke's hands once more and then tap the sergeant on the shoulder. "Ask the captain to run another question through his computer. Ask him how many of those fifteen places have booked wrestling for this Saturday?"

Duke gives you a thoughtful look and then passes your question along over the walkie-talkie.

The answer he gets back from the captain is, "*Just one:* the New York Sports Arena."

"Bingo!" cries Recondo.

"Nope... *wrestling*," you reply.

"And I thought you were barking up the wrong tree," says Mutt. His dog immediately starts to bark. "Not you," he says with exasperation to Junkyard. "Him!"

....

You're off to the Big Apple—and the core of COBRA's plot. Turn to page 68.

You decide to try a lasso. You make a loop at the end of your spare rope and quickly swing it out toward the boulder on the rock ledge. Your loop flies through the air ... and misses the boulder!

You've got time for just one more throw. But suddenly you get an inspiration. Instead of throwing your rope at the boulder, you throw it straight up toward the top of the cliff—and lasso Destro!

....
What a catch! Turn to page 18.

With your lasso around Destro and you hanging off the top of a cliff by a rope, both you and your enemy are in a tight spot.

"Drop your knife, Destro," you call out boldly, "because if I fall, you'll be right behind me! And if any of my buddies end up with their ropes cut," you add quickly, "you're still gonna come flying down to the bottom. So tell the Baroness and the rest of your playmates to drop their knives too...and back off!"

Will he do as you say? Turn to page 85.

You sprint down the underground corridor after your enemies. Destro and Storm Shadow aren't more than fifty feet in front of you, running slowly because of the sacks of meteor fragments they're carrying. Then they turn a corner. When you reach that same spot, your enemies have disappeared. In front of you are two stairways. One leads down into the building's boiler room, the other leads up to a higher level.

Which one do you think Destro and Storm Shadow took? The decision you make now could either save or doom the world. Good luck.

If you think Destro and Storm Shadow took the stairway down to the boiler room, turn to page 23.

If you think they took the stairs that lead up out of the basement, turn to page 31.

19

There must be at least thirty locals in front of you, armed with spears, bows and arrows, and blowguns.

But you didn't come to Blood Island to fight the natives. At least not if you can help it. Because you ran ahead of the others, though, you're going to have to make a split-second decision. Should you fight these natives or try to make peace with them? If you fight, you might lose because there are a lot of them and they are obviously ready to battle you. If you try to make peace and fail, you'll miss your chance to blast your way to safety.

Well, Outlaw, what's it going to be?

....
If you choose to fight it out with the natives, turn to page 35.

If you choose to try to make peace with them, turn to page 42.

21

"Destro and the others can't be that far ahead," you say. "And carrying all those rocks is bound to slow them up. Let's head out after them."

"Yeah," agrees Gung-Ho. "I'd love to sink my fists into that bunch."

You march off at a half run, following your enemies deeper and deeper into the jungle. After a short while Mutt's dog, Junkyard, picks up a scent and you let him lead the way. The trail is fresh and easy to follow, but somehow you just can't seem to catch up with Destro. He's keeping up a furious pace, in spite of the heavy rocks.

Turn to page 87.

Somehow, you have a hunch that Destro and Storm Shadow took the rocks down into the boiler room.

"If they're down there," you whisper to Snake-Eyes as you descend the staircase, "they've got no way out except right through us. So get ready."

The silent Snake-Eyes nods his understanding.

When you reach the bottom of the staircase, though, you don't see any sign of your enemies. The only thing that gets your attention is a small but thick cloud of steam hissing out of an open air vent.

It seems you made a mistake. Or did you?

You stare for a moment at the small cloud of steam and wonder why that air vent might have been left open. When you come up with a likely answer, you aim your auto pistol at the center of the cloud of steam and fire!

The bullet bounces off something hard! Of course! It hit a sack of meteor fragments! What else could make a bullet bounce? Now, out of the cloud of steam, comes a steaming mad Destro. He and Storm Shadow are carrying the meteor fragments in front of them for protection. And one of the sacks of rocks has a big bullet hole in it.

You keep firing but nothing can harm your enemies while they have those fragments to hide behind.

....

What next? Turn to page 24.

The action in the boiler room is about to get hot! Destro and Storm Shadow are charging right at you with the heavy sacks of meteor fragments. You square off to fight fairly, but your enemies suddenly heave the heavy bags of kiladeium at you.

"Eat dirt!" Destro yells.

Instinctively you reach out to catch them. That's what gives your two enemies a chance to race past you and up the stairs. They've escaped!

But you've got the meteor fragments and that's what counts! COBRA's plot has been defeated, thanks to you.

And from this day forward, anytime your boiler room victory is mentioned to Destro, he, well, boils with rage. So you'd better be careful the next time you open this book, or he just might get even. Today, however, you're the top soldier in the G.I. Joe unit. Enjoy the sweet taste of success—until your next adventure.

THE END

You quickly scout around the edge of the quicksand, looking for a suitable bamboo tree so you can get the Baroness out.

"Hurry!" the Baroness yells. "It's almost up to my chin!"

"It'd be a little quieter around here if it were over your mouth!" you answer back. A moment later you find a tree that looks sturdy enough for the job, and you bend it down until the Baroness can grab one of the branches.

You're just starting to ease the tree back up, pulling her out of the bog, when Mutt's dog barks a warning.

"Everybody hit the deck!" orders Duke.

Does that mean you too? If you let go of the bamboo tree, it'll snap up instantly and the Baroness will go flying as if she's been shot from a catapult. But if you're seen, you could draw fire on your teammates!

If you think you must let go of the bamboo tree, turn to page 36.

If you think you must hold onto the bamboo tree and risk being a possible target, turn to page 78.

You glance down the jungle path toward the COBRA ambush you've just avoided. "I think we should leave the Crimson Guards alone," you say. "For one thing, we're outnumbered...."

"So what?" says Gung-Ho. "We've fought that many before and won."

"Right," you admit, "but while they're sitting around waiting for us to blunder into their trap, we can get a head start on the rock search."

Duke backs you up, and the team heads down the new trail until the jungle comes to an abrupt end and you find yourselves at the edge of a big lake.

Duke takes out his map, looks at it, and then scratches his head. "That's funny," he says. "There isn't supposed to be a lake here."

While trying to decide what to do next, your scout, Recondo, reports back, saying that there are Crimson Guard patrols coming toward you from both the east and west sides of the lake. You're caught right between them!

What are you going to do?

"Get out your water wings," Duke says with a grim smile. "We gotta hide in this lake until those COBRA troopers are gone!"

....

Is Duke's plan all wet? Find out when you turn to page 80.

"Forget the retreat, boys," Duke says. "We're not going to let a little lava and fire scare us off. If we leave now we have no chance of ever getting those rocks. That means we can't go until we find that meteor."

You look around and find that the lava has slowed down and the fires aren't as bad as you thought they were, so everybody keeps cool.

Roadblock breaks the tension by joking, "We could roast some mighty fine marshmallows in that volcano."

"Marshmallows?" you say, playing along. "I didn't think you liked junk food. Only the best for you, I thought."

"Hey, marshmallows cooked over a hot volcano are a very rare delicacy, my friend," he jokes. "Can't get that just anywhere."

Everyone laughs, except the Baroness, and you continue on into the jungle for more than an hour. Finally, Recondo spots something that looks like a crater up ahead. The question is, who or what is going to get there first? You or the molten lava?

Or will it be COBRA Commander?

He and his Crimson Guards have just emerged from the jungle up ahead and to your right. And they're also heading straight for the crater!

....

You'd better move fast. Turn to page 47.

When you come to a fork in the trail, the Baroness smiles and says, "This way to the meteor crater." She takes the path on the right.

You tell yourself she must have found the landmark she was looking for.

But you haven't gone more than ten yards before the Baroness suddenly jumps off the trail and into the bushes. Before you can react, a hail of bullets rips the ground all around you.

"*Ambush!*" cries Duke.

Turn to page 40 and fight for your life!

You and your buddies stare doubtfully at the New York Sports Arena in front of you.

"Well, what do you think?" demands Gung-Ho. "Are we walking into a trap or not?"

"I don't know," Roadblock replies. "I just believe in setting a table properly, so that you know what all the courses are going to be. That's all."

What do *you* think? Is there a trap waiting for you in the crowded Sports Arena?

....
If you think you're walking into a trap, try to avoid it by turning to page 43.

If you think you've got the element of surprise on your side, turn to page 51.

You practically fly up that flight of stairs in pursuit of Destro and Storm Shadow, who have the meteor fragments. Just as you smash through the door at the top, you catch a glimpse of your enemies running down a long corridor. You're on the right trail!

Up and down several staircases and hallways you and Snake-Eyes run. Slowly, you gain on the two figures. At last you realize that you're on the building's main level, and up ahead you see your foes race into the packed wrestling arena!

You could very easily lose sight of Destro and Storm Shadow in that huge crowd of 25,000 screaming fans. But you have no choice. You've got to get those rocks!

Keep a sharp lookout for surprises and turn to page 84.

You and your G.I. Joe Team carefully search the dark tunnels beneath the Sports Arena. But you're not looking for Destro—at least not yet. Right now you're trying to find a suitable place to spring an ambush on any of the Crimson Guards foolish enough to be following you.

Suddenly, shattering the silence, a single gunshot booms out somewhere down a tunnel off to your left. On the heels of that, you hear the unmistakable voice of the Baroness crying out, "Destro, it's a trap!"

So Destro is here too. And it would seem that COBRA Commander plans to pay the infamous arms dealer his fee in blood! That's their business, though, not yours. All you want are those rocks! And now you know where they are. They're just down that tunnel. Run!

And keep running until you get to page 74.

If there's a chance she's telling the truth, you can't ignore it. But how are you going to get the meteor fragments if they are, in fact, at the bottom of the bog?

You glance around at the fellow members of your team...and your eyes settle on Blowtorch. That's it! Using his flamethrower, he can boil away the quicksand!

You clear your plan with Duke, and soon Blowtorch is hard at work. The bright yellow fire from his M-7 flamethrower starts the quicksand bubbling. Steam rises and slowly, ever so slowly, the level of the quicksand begins to go down. First it's just a few inches. Soon it's down by almost a foot!

But there's a long way to go. The jungle is hot enough, but now it's literally boiling. Trying to cool off, you absentmindedly slide out of your heavy backpack and drop it behind you.

Then, while you and the rest of the G.I. Joe Team have your attention squarely on the quicksand, the Baroness quietly drifts over to your abandoned pack, digs her hands inside, and pulls out a grenade!

Turn to page 65.

33

If the silence of the jungle was creepy, the wave of deafening sound that now rips through the air is positively terrifying. It takes you a minute before you realize what has happened. The volcano has erupted! The explosion knocks you off your feet, the entire island quaking from the shock of it.

And now the animals are no longer silent. Every living creature in the jungle is screaming with fear, racing away from the volcano. And with good reason. Molten lava is starting to flow down the side of the explosive mountain and into the jungle, setting the rain forest on fire!

You're all just getting to your feet when a pack of crazed jungle cats comes racing down the trail right toward you. Their teeth are bared and you know that they'll kill anything standing in their way. The problem is, *you're* in their way!

You could draw your weapons and try shooting them, but if you miss even a few, your team will get terribly mauled. Your other alternative is for all of you to lie as flat as you can. There's a small chance that when the cats run by they won't stop to bite you or, more of a problem, that their sharp claws won't rip you to shreds as they race over your bodies.

The cats are almost on top of you....

....

If you choose to shoot, turn to page 39.

If you choose to risk lying flat and hope for the best, turn to page 54.

34

The native army is getting restless. In one quick movement you grab a stun grenade off your belt and throw it right into the middle of the native warriors. Then you hit the deck.

Arrows and spears zing over your head until you finally hear the explosion that knocks a dozen of the locals out cold. And by then Recondo, Gung-Ho, and the others are streaming out of the cave, joining the fight and tossing one stun grenade after another at the natives.

It isn't long before practically all of the Blood Island warriors are lying on the ground, unconscious. But one of them is still wide awake—and hanging on for dear life at the top of a rubber tree. Mutt and his dog, Junkyard, are at the bottom of that tree and the warrior is scared stiff.

Duke orders Mutt and Junkyard to let the man down and then asks the frightened warrior about the meteor that struck his island. The answer that Duke gets doesn't make any of you very happy.

....

To find out what the warrior said, turn to page 55.

35

There's no way you're going to sacrifice yourself for the Baroness. Besides, she's already up to her mouth in quicksand, so she seems like a goner even if you don't let go of the bamboo tree she's holding on to.

"Sorry!" you shout as you let go of the tree and drop to the ground with your auto pistol in your hand.

The tree snaps up just as you knew it would, and you figure that's the end of the Baroness. Strange, though, that you didn't hear her scream. She must have been awfully tough, you think to yourself.

But that's all the thinking you've got time for. The bushes at the edge of the clearing start to move and you know that whoever is coming will be bursting into the clearing in about three seconds.

Don't look at your watch, just turn to page 50.

This is insane, you think to yourself. We're letting the *Baroness* lead us through some heaven-forsaken jungle to who knows where!

At a fork in the trail, the Baroness smiles and says, "This way to the meteor crater." Then she starts off to her right.

"Wait a minute," you order.

"What's the matter?" she asks innocently.

"We're not going that way. We're taking the trail to the left."

"But that won't lead you to the meteor crater," she argues.

"I'll take that risk."

Duke comes up behind you and asks, "You know what you're doing, Outlaw?"

"I think so, but just to be sure, why don't you have Recondo scout around that trail the Baroness wants us to take."

"Good idea."

Fifteen minutes later, Recondo races back with a look of relief on his face. "There must be a full division of Crimson Guards up that trail," he reports. "We would've been dead meat if we'd gone that way!"

The Baroness has been lying all along. It's better that you found out now, though, rather than when the whole COBRA army was using you for target practice. But now you need a new strategy.

Make your next move on page 79.

With the volcano erupting, the jungle in flames, and a pack of hysterical jungle cats racing toward you, you stand up straight and tall, draw your weapons to shoot and—you're way too slow. The big cats leap at you in a mad frenzy of fear, tearing at you with sharp, flashing teeth.

Bad choice, Outlaw. You lose. In fact, you might say you've just suffered a cat-astrophe!

THE END

You've walked right into the Baroness's trap! A bullet rips a hole in your jungle hat, giving you a new, unexpected part in your hair. Recondo gets wounded in the shoulder, Roadblock takes a slug in the leg, and there's blood on Duke's forehead from a bullet that grazed him.

But you're the most highly trained military outfit in the world. Even when caught flat-footed, a G.I. Joe Team never loses its discipline. Despite your wounds, you quickly form into a fighting unit with one goal—survival!

You throw as much lead as you can at the ambushers and then perform a perfect rearguard action to protect your retreat, dragging your hostage, the Baroness, with you.

As soon as you're out of range, though, you've got to pick up and run! "Get as much distance between them and us as possible!" Duke yells, leading you in a mad race against death.

Out of breath and bleeding, you make your own trail through the thick jungle. It's getting dark but you keep running as hard and as fast as you can...until suddenly your entire team falls head over heels into a deep pit!

....

Have you landed in another trap? You'll find out when you turn to page 88.

The thought of a slow, painful death from swimming in toxic water makes you yearn for whatever trouble the Crimson Guards have waiting for you on shore. Quickly you signal the others and lead them back up toward the surface.

Was the lake really full of a toxic chemical? You'll never know, because when your team breaks above the water line, the Crimson Guards spot you instantly and open fire. Within a few seconds, all of you are doing the dead-man's float.

You made a bad choice. Even if there was a slow-acting poison in the water, wouldn't that have been a lot better than a fast-acting bullet?

THE END

You raise your right hand in a universal gesture of peace. The response the natives give you is just as universally understood: it's a poison blowgun dart in your neck!

Nice try, but now you're destined for a very small hat size.

Close the book. You may open it again only after you look into a mirror and see that you no longer have a shrunken head.

THE END

Playing it safe, you enter the huge indoor arena through an alley door. You can't hear the fans screaming back here. Everything is quiet, and the only sound to break the silence is the shallow breathing of your team.

Feeling your way through the dark, you soon find yourselves at the entrance to an old abandoned elevator shaft. You look toward the bottom—nearly one hundred feet down—and see a faint light below.

"The only thing that could possibly be down there is COBRA headquarters," you whisper to Duke.

He nods his agreement.

You've hit pay dirt!

There's an old but sturdy-looking elevator cable leading down the shaft. Each of you in turn jumps out into the shaft, grabs the cable, and slowly begins to climb down toward the light. When you're all assembled at the bottom of the dark shaft, you take out your weapons and get set to make your move.

Are you ready for action? Turn to page 66.

You, Snake-Eyes, Destro, and Storm Shadow are about to clobber each other in a wrestling ring in front of 25,000 spectators. The ring announcer doesn't have the slightest idea who any of you are, but he thinks fast and his booming voice fills the arena. "This is a tag-team bout. One fall, winner take all."

The bell sounds and Storm Shadow strides into the center of the ring. You know better than to take on an eighth-degree black belt. Instead, Snake-Eyes goes out to meet him. They've studied martial arts with the same Ninja family and the battle is furious—but it isn't anything like wrestling. It's the most incredible kung fu exhibition these fans have ever seen! And they're eating it up—until Destro sneaks into the ring and hits Snake-Eyes from behind! It looks as if your enemies are not only going to pin Snake-Eyes, they're going to kill him! The fans' cheers turn to loud boos.

But in the next instant you jump into the ring and knock Destro down with a flying drop kick. Now the fans are cheering you!

Destro picks himself up off the canvas. There's fire in his eyes and you know that one of you won't leave this ring alive.

....

You've wrestled yourself into this, now let's see if you can wrestle yourself out. Turn to page 82.

You've just saved the Baroness from an untimely burial in jungle quicksand. But you're sure that doesn't matter to her. She'd lie her teeth out as long as she could get a pair of dentures.

"You know what I think?" you say to the Baroness.

"No, what?" she sneers.

"I think COBRA Commander sent you here to keep us busy on a wild-goose chase. He'd just love for us to spend precious time digging down into this quicksand pit for something that isn't even there."

"You're out of your mind," says the Baroness.

"Am I? Well then, why don't you show us where the meteor crater is? According to your story, you've already been there. If you can lead us to the crater, it'll prove you're telling the truth. And if that's so, then we can come back here later and somehow get to those rocks at the bottom of the bog."

"Sure," she says, "I'll show you how to get to the crater." There's the hint of a smile on her face ... and that worries you.

Follow the Baroness to page 77.

This could turn out to be one strange little jungle party. It looks like you, the Crimson Guards, and a stream of deadly molten lava are going to reach that meteor crater at exactly the same moment!

"Double-time!" shouts Duke, and the team sets off at a sprint toward the crash site.

COBRA Commander sees you and orders his troops to stop and open fire. That's a big mistake, because his army might have gotten to the crater first if he hadn't slowed them down to shoot at you.

With bullets whizzing over your heads, your whole team jumps down into the big hole in the ground that was made by the meteor.

"Whew, that was close," you say, fingering a smooth rock made of solid kiladeium. But then you look up and see burning lava flowing on a path that will send it right over the top of the crater. If you stay here for another three minutes, you'll be burned alive in a stew of molten rock!

You're stuck, until you turn to page 56.

Loaded down with meteor fragments, you and your buddies each grab hold of the rope and start climbing out of the crater and across the stream of lava. The heat rising from the molten rock beneath you is almost suffocating, but you keep on going.

Roadblock is doing his job, keeping up a steady stream of machine-gun fire, and the Crimson Guards can't get off a clean shot at you.

But when you're halfway across the river of lava, it suddenly starts to get wider. You watch in horror as it spreads out toward the big rubber tree that's holding the other end of the rope.

It gets closer and closer to the tree. All of you climb as fast as you can, hand over hand, hand over hand, hand over hand. You're almost across . . . but it's too late! The lava touches the tree and it instantly bursts into flames. The rope disintegrates from the heat. For an instant you and the rest of the team are left grabbing at thin air. Then, it's into the boiling lava for all of you.

Well, look at it this way—at least COBRA didn't get the meteor fragments. Maybe you didn't win, but then again, you didn't lose. The next time you open this book, though, you'll have a burning desire to bring even more glory to the name of G.I Joe.

THE END

With your guns raised and ready, you burst into the clearing...only to find you've been tricked! A wild pig with a Crimson Guard uniform tied around its neck turns around and looks at you as if to say, "Why are you guys following me?"

Good question.

It seems as if Mutt and his dog found the stink of COBRA Commander's lackeys even stronger than the pig's. And because of that, Destro will link up with COBRA Commander and they'll hog all the meteor fragments. That's what happens when you make a pig-headed decision.

THE END

The clearing is still, but you're sure something fierce is about to go down. Junkyard, Mutt's dog, is barking like crazy now. That's not like him. Usually he quiets down once he's sounded the alarm.

But a second later you find out why he won't shut up. A female poodle trots out of the jungle and starts yapping at something in the quicksand. You look back over your shoulder and see ... the Baroness! You can't help yourself, you're relieved!

"What are you still doing here?" you ask.

"I let go of the tree just before you did," she replies angrily. "I didn't want to learn how to fly. Now how about getting me out of here before my little poodle attacks and kills all of you brave soldier boys."

"Okay, okay," you answer with just a touch of embarrassment. This time, rather than bend the bamboo tree back, you figure you'll just throw her a rope after all.

....
This could be some tug-of-war. Turn to page 62.

50

"I don't think the arena meeting is a trap," you announce decisively. "COBRA Commander wants those rocks more than he wants us right now. I don't think he'd waste time setting us up until he got the meteor fragments from Destro."

"I'll back you up on that one," says Duke.

"So where do we look first?" asks Gung-Ho, getting ready for action.

"Well, the arena is full of wrestling fans," Recondo points out.

"Maybe *underneath* the arena," you suggest.

"Sure," Duke says, "that's the only logical place for Destro and COBRA Commander to meet."

So it's into the bowels of the building you go.

You're looking for bad guys but, without realizing it, you accidentally trip a warning device and help COBRA Commander find *you*. You turn a corner and find yourself in a pipe-lined corridor—face to face with your enemy.

How are you going to get out of this one? Turn to page 52 and find out.

"Drop your weapons or die!" COBRA Commander demands. It's not an idle threat. He's backed up by at least fifty heavily armed Crimson Guards, and there's no escape route in the narrow corridor.

You look around quickly and see that Destro is nowhere in sight. You beat him to the rendezvous point. That means COBRA Commander may not know the fate of the kiladeium. If that's true, maybe you can bluff your way out of this.

But if you think a bluff won't work, you've got to create a diversion—and fast. You're sure you could bust open one of these pipes and then try to escape.

Which plan will work? Hurry! Choose before COBRA Commander starts shooting!

If you think your best chance for escape is to try bluffing COBRA Commander, turn to page 64.

If you think you should try to create a diversion by puncturing one of the pipes, turn to page 58.

52

As you wait to open fire on the unsuspecting Crimson Guards, the seconds seem endless. Then Duke simultaneously pulls the trigger of his Colt and yells, *"Open fire!"*

Your G.I. Joe Team blasts the enemy. Bullets scream through the air, grenades send shrapnel flying. It isn't pretty, but it sure is effective.

The Crimson Guard forces—what's left of them—flee across the trail, practically trampling the other COBRA troops waiting there.

With COBRA's army in retreat, Duke gives your team the order to pull out.

Quickly, the team heads back to the other trail, bringing the Baroness, still bound, as a prisoner. You march farther into the dark tropical rain forest, looking for the meteor crater. But as you tromp through the heavy undergrowth, you notice something very peculiar. It's completely silent. There isn't a single sound in the jungle, no birds cawing, no insects buzzing, no animals to be seen at all. There's nothing. It's as if the whole jungle is holding its breath, waiting for something to happen. And then it does!

Get ready for it on page 34.

With lava running toward you and the jungle burning down around your ears, you're almost as scared as the huge jungle cats that are about to mow you down. Only one choice.... You hug the ground, and the cats, wild to put as much distance as they can between themselves and the exploding volcano, leap over your bodies without so much as touching you!

The danger seems to have passed, but then you find it's only just begun. Hot ash starts falling out of the sky and the volcano erupts once again, sending even more lava down its slope.

"We've got to get out of here!" cries the Baroness, who is still your prisoner.

All eyes turn to Duke. He's the leader and it's his decision.

....
What does Duke say? Find out on page 27.

With all his friends knocked out by your stun grenades, the native warrior is willing to talk. Using sign language and some English he's picked up from explorers, he tells you, "A great rock came falling out of the sky and made a giant hole in the ground. This place of wonder is close by, but others of your kind have already been there."

"What others?" asks Duke, fearing he already knows what the native will say.

"There were many," replies the warrior, "but the two leaders were a man with a silver face and a woman who wore circles around her eyes. The others were the color of blood."

Duke scowls. Destro, the Baroness, and the Crimson Guards have gotten to the meteor first.

You've got to find their trail and catch up with them before they get off the island. It's your only chance! If Destro ever links up with COBRA Commander and sells him the kiladeium, you might just as well not bother going home.

· ·

You haven't a second to lose. Hurry and turn to page 63.

55

Snake-Eyes wastes no time. He quickly blasts a canal out of the jungle floor and the lava is forced to take a new course, flowing around the far side of the crater. That buys you some time, but now you're stuck inside the crater. You've got lava on one side and COBRA on the other!

Sure, you've finally got the rocks, but how are you going to get away with them?

You're in a hopeless situation—and COBRA Commander knows it. Using a bullhorn, he calls out to you, offering a trade. "I'll let you live," he announces, "if you leave the rocks. Just drop your weapons and no harm will come to you."

"Right," you mutter sarcastically, "and Tinkerbell will rescue us!" Obviously you can't trust COBRA Commander. But what choices do you have? You can either try to trick your enemy somehow, or you can figure out a way to cross the river of lava and escape.

Hey, if it was easy, everybody would be a G.I. Joe. This is it. Make your decision!

If you try to trick COBRA, turn to page 61.

If you try to cross the river of lava, turn to page 67.

If the lake is poisoned, you may be dying right now! But if you swim to the surface, the Crimson Guards will certainly kill you at once. So you keep on diving deeper and deeper.

With fear bubbling in your stomach, you head for the very center of the bottom of the lake. When you get there, you suddenly realize the incredible truth!

The lake isn't poisoned at all. In fact, it isn't even really a lake. *This is the meteor crater!* It all makes perfect sense to you now. No wonder this body of water wasn't on Duke's map. No wonder there's no life here. This huge hole in the ground was created just a few days ago. It filled with water that ran off from the mountains above the jungle.

You've realized all this because you've spotted the meteor fragments. They don't look like any rocks you've ever seen before, so that *must* be what they are!

And you're right!

You and the others gather the precious rocks in a carefully organized underwater operation. When the sun goes down, you head for shore. Then, under the cover of night, you slip back toward the beach, signal the submarine, and head for home. How do you like being a hero?

THE END

COBRA Commander seems to be holding all the cards. But as Duke and the rest of the team begin to lay down their guns, you lean against one of the pipes—one that seems real hot to the touch. You hold your auto pistol right up against it, hidden from view, and pull the trigger!

You jump out of the way as a scalding spray of steam shoots out of the pipe and showers over COBRA Commander and his henchmen. Yelling and screaming, they stumble back out of the way while the sheet of white-hot steam completely blocks their vision.

Your teammates immediately jump into action. They scoop their weapons up off the floor and make a mad scramble back down the corridor as bullets fired blindly by the angry Crimson Guards whistle over your heads.

Though you manage to get away, you still don't have the meteor fragments. Destro is the one who holds the key to those rocks, but where is he?

Maybe you'll find out when you turn to page 32.

Destro throws himself off the ropes of the wrestling ring, his full weight hurtling toward you! But you roll out of his way just in time, and he hits the empty canvas like a diver doing a belly flop.

In a killing rage, Destro gets up and races to his corner. You watch, horrified, as he reaches down to pick up a sack of rocks. He's going to use them as a weapon against you!

The fans are outraged and they're booing Destro even more loudly than before. At this moment he's the most hated man in wrestling. And the most dangerous. You've got to stop him or you're a goner.

You can try to head off Destro's attack with a quickly executed flying-scissor lock. Or you can wait until he gets his hands on the rocks and then hit him with a grand slam.

What are you going to do?

....

If you choose to try the flying-scissor lock, turn to page 69.

If you choose to try the grand slam, turn to page 70.

60

Trapped with the rocks in the meteor crater by COBRA Commander and a stream of boiling lava, you come up with a desperate plan. Its success depends on whether or not you can convince COBRA Commander that you're actually going to take him up on his offer. But he knows you're suspicious of him. He'd never believe that you'd actually trust him. So you've got to establish a deal that genuinely guarantees he'll keep his end of the bargain.

The first thing you do is gag the Baroness again so she can't warn her leader. Then you quickly fill up a couple of bags with worthless stones blown into the crater when the volcano exploded.

Once you've done all that, Duke calls out to COBRA Commander, "Okay, we've thought it over and you've got a deal. But we'll do it our way or not at all. We'll leave the Baroness with the rocks, but we're setting a remote-control bomb next to the lava canal. The Baroness stays here with the rocks. If you shoot at us, *kaboom* goes the bomb and the lava flows over your friend and the kiladeium. In other words, COBRA Commander, if you try to pull a fast one, you'll end up with absolutely nothing. Do we have a deal?"

....

Will COBRA Commander believe you? Find out on page 73.

By now the Baroness is up to her neck in quicksand. "Grab hold of this!" you yell as you throw her a long rope. You hold the other end tight, ready to pull her out of the bog. She takes the rope in both of her hands...and then gives it a sharp jerk. Which is what you are—a jerk—because she catches you off balance and pulls you into the quicksand, headfirst!

Now you're in over your head in trouble—and quicksand. The Baroness is just kneeling on the edge of the bog. She isn't actually in it—but you are...*glug*...*glug*...*glug*. We've got a sinking feeling this is...

THE END

You've just got to catch Destro, the Baroness, and the Crimson Guards. The team heads for the top of the cliff where you last saw them. Recondo's like a human bloodhound in the jungle and it doesn't take him long to pick up the trail. You're about to set off after your enemies into the mass of towering trees when the team receives a radio transmission from the submarine off the island's coast.

"Picked up a coded message from COBRA Commander to Destro," says a navy radio expert. "Deciphered it, but it still doesn't make much sense. Maybe you can figure it out. Here it is: 'Wrestle rocks to Saturday's 25,000 screamers.'"

How important is that message? Will stopping to figure it out make it easier for you to find Destro? Or will stopping now make it impossible for you to ever catch up with the evil people who have those precious meteor fragments?

....

If you choose to stop and try to figure out the message, turn to page 14.

If you choose to ignore the message and keep going after Destro, turn to page 22.

63

You're in a pretty bad position. COBRA Commander and fifty Crimson Guards are about to turn you into Swiss cheese. You've got no choice but to bluff them.

"Just hold on there, you slippery little snake in the grass," you challenge boldly. "Before you start shooting off that gun or worse, your mouth," you say as if you're holding all the aces, "there's something you ought to know."

"And what might that be?" asks the suspicious leader of COBRA.

"We've already tangled with Destro and we've got the meteor fragments," you announce.

"If that's true," he slowly replies, "what are you doing here?"

He's taken the bait. You were hoping he'd say that. "Like I said, we tangled with Destro and we've got the kiladeium. But Destro captured one of our team. We came here to make a trade. The rocks for our friend."

Behind that faceless evil, a brain is working. COBRA Commander wants those meteor fragments and now he sees a way to get them.

"Perhaps we can work something out," he says, lowering his weapon. The Crimson Guards follow their leader's example. This is your chance!

....

Seize the moment. Turn to page 83.

At that moment a mosquito bites you on the back of the neck, and when you swipe at it your head turns just enough to catch a glimpse of the Baroness. Your eyes bulge wide when you see her pull the pin of a grenade and throw it in your direction!

The grenade bounces once and rolls to a stop right at your feet! There's a five-second timer on that grenade and at least two seconds have already gone by.

Should you try to pick it up and throw it into the jungle before it explodes, or should you try to kick it into the quicksand? Not only your life, but the lives of your fellow team members are in your hands.

You've got less than three seconds...two seconds....

If you try to pick up the grenade and throw it into the jungle, turn to page 72.

If you try to kick the grenade into the quicksand, turn to page 75.

Before you can step away from the bottom of the elevator shaft, there's a sudden change in the air. You can sense it but you don't know what it is. And then it hits you...literally! Right on the head!

Destro is delivering his heavy sacks of rocks from Blood Island by throwing them down the old elevator shaft!

No one knew you were coming. In fact, no one will even know you were here until they dig you out from underneath two tons of meteor fragments.

You really got rocked to sleep. For good! Next time—if you have the courage for a next time—don't be so cautious. Just charge straight ahead and hope that you come to a better...

END

No way are you going to trust COBRA Commander to let you live once you've left the meteor fragments in the crater. He'd kill you all in a second if he had the chance. Your only choice is to try to escape from the pit over the stream of burning lava.

Duke orders Snake-Eyes to swing a rope high up onto the trunk of a thick rubber tree on the other side of the river of burning lava.

"We're climbing across, hand over hand," Duke announces.

"This may be a stupid question," says Mutt, "but what's to keep COBRA from shooting us off that rope like ducks in a shooting gallery?"

"Roadblock is staying behind with his machine gun to keep the Crimson Guards pinned down so they can't fire at us," he replies.

"But then how is Roadblock going to get across?" you ask, worried about the fate of your friend.

"No problem," says Duke. "After we get across with the kiladeium, COBRA Commander isn't going to care about Roadblock. He'll be busy trying to find a way to cut us off before we reach the beach and leave the island. Roadblock can catch up to us later."

That's the plan. Do you think it will work?

You won't know until you start climbing. Get a good grip on that rope and turn to page 48!

You leave the tropical jungle by submarine and head straight for the concrete jungle. It's already Saturday night when you get to New York City so you waste no time racing over to the Sports Arena, which is by now filled with screaming wrestling fans.

When you arrive there, Roadblock surprises everyone by quietly announcing, "I wonder if COBRA *wanted* us to intercept that message."

Gung-Ho stares, a look of horror on his face, and asks, "You think it's some kind of setup?"

"Could be," Roadblock replies. "It has, shall I say, the delicate taste and the heady aroma of a carefully seasoned COBRA trap."

"In other words," you translate, "you think we're about to get our gooses cooked."

Roadblock smiles. "I couldn't have put it any better myself."

....

Is COBRA about to eat you alive? Turn to page 30 and find out.

68

Just as Destro lifts the bag of rocks to bean you, you jump at him, both legs aimed straight for his neck. It would have been a beautiful flying-scissor lock. But unfortunately for you, Destro knows the perfect counter move to your attack. He drops down to his back and kicks up at you as you go sailing by. You end up flying right out of the ring—and right out of the book!

With the bag of rocks in his hands, Destro smashes Snake-Eyes over the head. Storm Shadow and Destro leave the ring under a hail of boos and catcalls. The fans may not like them, but they've won the match. More important than that, *they* have the meteor fragments, which means they'll soon hold the world at their mercy.

And what do you have? Thousands of true-blue wrestling fans, and a chance to open this book again and get the kiladeium. Be there! We're counting on you.

THE END

It's a fight to the finish, you against Destro in New York's biggest wrestling arena. There's only one move to go for—the grand slam! You hold back for just a second as Destro takes hold of the sack full of meteor fragments. At that moment, when his hands are no longer free, you dive into a forward somersault. The whipping motion of your body builds up speed. You swing your legs up halfway through your roll, kicking out. And you hit Destro square in the chest with the heels of your feet! He falls back toward the ropes, dropping the bag of rocks. When you finish your somersault, you come up with both fists ready. You hit him with a wicked one-two punch combination to his stomach. You've clobbered him with both feet and both fists—it's a grand slam! Destro sinks to the canvas, totally beaten!

The crowd goes wild! Thousands of fans swarm down the aisles and into the ring. A grin crosses your swollen face as you see Storm Shadow and Destro swept up into the crowd—away from their precious kiladeium. You get some of your ecstatic fans to help you carry the meteor fragments as they carry you out of the ring on their shoulders. Yo, Joe! You're not only a hero, you're a star!

THE END

You dive to the ground, grab the live grenade in your right hand, cock your arm to throw it, and...

BOOM!

The grenade blows up in your hand and you end up in as many fragments as the meteor that struck the island.

This was a bad time to go to pieces. Close the book and pull yourself together!

THE END

While you wait for COBRA Commander's answer, seconds tick away and the lava flows even closer to the crater where you're trapped. You all stuff the meteor fragments into your clothes and backpacks. You make sure there's no visible evidence that you're carrying away the real rocks.

Finally COBRA Commander gives you his answer. "I'm surprised," he says through his bull-horn. "I really thought you'd try some impossible escape across the lava. But I must say, it's quite clever of you to hold both the Baroness and the meteor fragments hostage. You're quite right in assuming that if I had the chance, I'd kill every one of you. But," he laughs, "I suppose I'll just have to let you live the rest of your lives in shame. After all, you'll be responsible for letting me become the most powerful man on earth! So save your miserable skins. I agree to your conditions!"

"Nice speech, huh?" Mutt says with a smile.

Duke grins. "It's nothing compared to the speech he's going to make when he finds out we've fooled him." Then he turns to all of you and says, "Come on, let's roll."

"You mean *rock* and roll," you offer with a laugh. And sure enough, you get away, because you've got the beat that beat COBRA!

THE END

Without a moment to lose, you dash down the narrow corridors underneath the New York Sports Arena. Destro, the Baroness, and the rocks are, at the moment, being held by the double-crossing COBRA Commander.

Turning a corner, you almost run right into the backs of a battalion of Crimson Guards. They've surrounded Destro and the Baroness, and COBRA Commander is ordering his lackeys to pick up the sacks of kiladeium.

Duke doesn't hesitate. "Start blasting!" he yells. You fire a massive volley that tears through COBRA's ranks. All your M-16s are set on full automatic and the lead is flying everywhere!

Turn to page 86.

"Live grenade!" you shout as you kick the explosive device into the middle of the bog. You and the rest of the team dive to the ground. The grenade splashes into the quicksand and begins to sink.

But not for long.

Suddenly there's a huge explosion! Hundreds of gallons of quicksand are sent hurtling into the air in every direction. When it comes down, it's like a thick rain of goop. All of you are covered with it.

But the bog is empty . . . except for the heavy sack of meteor fragments lying on the bottom. You've got them! And only at the cost of having to take a bath!

THE END

As you hurtle through the gloomy hallway toward Destro, the Baroness, Storm Shadow, and the fragments, you get ready with your M-16. "Drop those rocks and raise your hands!" you shout, thinking you've got the rest of the G.I. Joe Team right behind you. But they never heard your instructions. It's just you and Snake-Eyes!

"Wipe them out," Destro calmly orders the Crimson Guards who are with him.

The COBRA soldiers raise their weapons, but they're slow to fire. And you're not about to give them a helping hand. You let go with a burst of automatic fire from your M-16. Death rips across the front line of Crimson Guards.

"I'm getting out of here!" the Baroness yells, and what's left of the COBRA soldiers follow her, running for their lives.

Destro and Storm Shadow also make a run for it. But they're not fleeing empty-handed. They've taken the sacks of precious meteor fragments and they're getting away!

Quick. Keep after them. Turn to page 19.

76

Before you let the Baroness lead you to the meteor crater, you tie her hands behind her back. Keeping a gun trained on the middle of her back, you say, "Lead on, Baroness."

She turns and grins at you as she answers, "Nothing could give me more pleasure."

With the Baroness showing you the way, you and the rest of the G.I. Joe Team head deeper into the jungle.

After an hour of hacking away at the overgrown trail, you ask the Baroness, "How much farther until we reach the crater?"

"It won't be long now," she replies as she glances nervously into the bushes on either side of the trail.

She's searching for something. But what? Could it be a signal from someone who's going to ambush you? Or is she just looking for a landmark?

···
If you think you're being led into an ambush, don't take the next turn the Baroness suggests. Take the turn to page 37 instead.

If you think the Baroness is simply looking for a landmark, follow her directly to page 28.

"I can't believe this ridiculous situation I've gotten myself into," you mutter. Things couldn't get much worse. You're hanging onto a bamboo tree, trying to get one of your worst enemies out of a pit of quicksand, and you're a sitting duck for whatever is hiding in the jungle at the edge of the clearing.

A spear sails out of the undergrowth and digs into the ground just inches from your feet. A second later, a whole tribe of native warriors—there must be at least fifty of them—come charging out of the jungle. An arrow zings into the tree trunk just above your hands.

You're all set to let go of the bamboo tree when Duke and the rest of your G.I. Joe Team send a hail of bullets over the heads of the natives. They don't want to kill them, just scare them off.

The natives have never seen firepower before. The noise alone is deafening and instantaneously they break off their attack and run back into the jungle.

The battle is over almost as quickly as it began. And there are no casualties—although you came awfully close.

Now it's time to find out if saving the Baroness was worth risking your life.

....

Want to learn what the Baroness knows? Turn to page 4.

You glance around the jungle, wondering what the team's next move should be. Then Gung-Ho pipes up with a suggestion. "Let's get 'em! Let's ambush the ambushers! If we knock out COBRA's main force, it'll slow down their search for the meteor crater."

"I say we stay as far away from those Crimson Guards as possible," counters Mutt. "We didn't come here to fight, we came here to get those rocks."

Which do you think is the right choice?

....

If you think you should ambush the ambushers, turn to page 6.

If you think you should put all your effort into finding the meteor crater, turn to page 26.

With Crimson Guards coming at you from both sides, you have no choice but to follow Duke's orders and go for an unexpected swim in the strange lake you've found. You dive into the cold, clear water and head for the bottom. As you swim farther and farther down into the depths, you notice something strange. There are no fish in this lake. In fact there is no life of any kind, no plants, no coral... there's just sand and stone.

What if the water is poisoned? What if you're absorbing some toxic chemical through your skin with every second you spend in this lake?

You've got a tough decision to make. If you believe that swimming in this water is dangerous, you've got to head back to shore immediately and risk facing the Crimson Guards. Your other choice is to trust that your fears are wrong and keep swimming toward the bottom of the lake, where the Crimson Guards can't see you.

Which will you risk, death above or death below?

If you think you should return to the shore immediately, turn to page 41.

If you think you should keep swimming for the bottom of the lake, turn to page 57.

Destro dives at your legs, but you jump up over his outstretched arms and come down on his back with a knee drop. Any ordinary man would be yelling in agony—but Destro is no ordinary man. He turns over on his side and grabs a handful of your hair and flips you—head-first—over onto your back.

You lie there motionless, the wind knocked out of you. Destro thinks you're badly hurt, so he climbs up on the ropes. He's about to leap down on top of you with a vicious cannonball death jump.

Are you dead meat? Turn to page 60.

COBRA Commander bought your bluff. The Crimson Guards have lowered their weapons.

Wham! You pull out your auto pistol and start blasting. The rest of the G.I. Joe Team is right behind you, firing their M-16s. Bullets ricochet off the walls, making your volley as deadly as the fire from a full battalion. You've turned the tables on COBRA and now they're on the run!

"Good work!" Duke calls out to you as you race down the corridor, trying to capture COBRA Commander. But just then something catches your eye. It's the glint of light on a shiny surface. You stop and peer into a long, dark hallway. It takes a few seconds, but your eyes soon grow accustomed to the light—and that's when you recognize what's in the gloom. It's Destro!

The light was shining on his mask.

With him are the Baroness, Storm Shadow, COBRA's Ninja bodyguard, and several Crimson Guards. But far more important, Destro has the meteor fragments!

Catching COBRA Commander doesn't matter anymore. It's those rocks that count. "G.I. Joes!" you shout. "This way!" And without looking back over your shoulder to see how many of your fellow soldiers heard you, you dash down the dark hallway toward Destro and the kiladeium. And toward an unknown fate.

....

Turn to page 76.

83

As it turns out, there's no way you're going to lose sight of Destro and Storm Shadow because the screaming fans in the arena think that all four of you are wrestlers!

It's a case of mistaken identities, but at least this way Destro and Storm Shadow can't hide. Cheering and applauding all the while, the crowd opens a pathway that leads straight to the ring.

Destro and Storm Shadow are pushed up through the ropes. They try to protest but the crowd thinks it's all part of the show. The whole arena seems to throb with the foot-stomping, whistling, and yelling of the fans. Destro eats it up. He's probably never been cheered before!

He bows to the crowd and they cheer even louder. He was planning to make a run for it, but why should he now? He's a hero, right?

"Put down that sack," Destro tells Storm Shadow, "and get ready to wrestle these two weaklings to the death!"

Well, the fans might think Destro's a hero, but you know better. "Come on, Snake-Eyes!" you shout as you climb into the ring too. "At least if we fight these jokers in the ring, innocent people won't get hurt."

Flex your muscles and turn to page 45.

Destro knows your reputation, Outlaw, so he can be sure you're not bluffing. He orders the others to drop their knives, and they do.

Meanwhile, you and the rest of the G.I. Joe Team climb up to the top of the cliff. Roadblock trains his machine gun on the Baroness and the Crimson Guards. Then, noticing what else is on the top of the cliff, he lets out a low whistle. "*Oo-ee*, would you look at this!" Big, heavy sacks full of rocks are strewn all around.

"Seems like these jokers have saved us a lot of work," you say with a laugh. "How nice of them to find the meteor fragments and stash them in these bags for us!"

The taste of victory is sweet. With the kiladeium in your possession and a rope around Destro, you've brought your mission to a sudden and spectacular end. Yo, Joe!

THE END

In the blood and gunsmoke, you see COBRA Commander try to sneak away with the heavy sacks of rocks. You leap over three Crimson Guards and smash into his back. He drops the sacks and goes flying, but he isn't ready to let you have those rocks. He pulls a knife out of his cloak and cocks his arm to throw it at you.

"Go ahead and try it!" you snarl at him as you draw your auto pistol.

COBRA Commander looks death right in the face—and he doesn't like what he sees. He dives into an open sewer and disappears with a splash. Too bad he didn't know you'd already emptied your auto pistol on his Crimson Guards.

Though COBRA Commander got away, *you* have the meteor fragments. Your G.I. Joe Team got the rare element by using that other rare element—surprise. Congratulations! You may get a "metal" for this.

THE END

After twenty-four hours of slogging through the dense jungle, you finally hear something up ahead. You're at the point of exhaustion but there's no question about it. It's got to be Destro, fighting through the jungle undergrowth.

You pull out your weapons and get ready for battle. "They must have a helicopter waiting for them!" Duke yells. "Under no circumstances can we let them get to it!"

You hear the sounds of branches breaking dead ahead. Something else will soon be dead—and it might be you.

There! Movement in the clearing, right through the trees! Hurry!

Sprint to page 49.

What is this huge pit doing in the middle of the jungle? you wonder, hoping desperately you and your wounded buddies aren't goners this time.

Stunned by your fall, you lie at the bottom of the pit and try to catch your breath. When you finally begin to roll over and get to your feet, a sharp stone digs into your side. You reach down to push it away, but the feel of the rock in your hands makes you stop.

"Duke!" you call out.

"What?"

Before you can answer, you start laughing like a lunatic.

"What's gotten into him?" asks Gung-Ho.

"Don't know," says Blowtorch. "Sounds like he's lost his marbles."

"Outlaw!" demands Duke. "What's the matter?"

"The matter?" you crow. "The matter? Nothing's the matter! You know that meteor crater we've been searching high and low for? Well, we've just fallen into it!"

When you show the guys the meteor fragment in your hand, they start laughing like crazy along with you!

You're still laughing when you're safely on board the submarine. You did it! Operation Death Stone is a rousing success...thanks to *you*, Outlaw.

THE END